THE
WRONG

THE WRONG

CARMEN CAMBRIDGE

COPYRIGHT

To the good Samaritan

Contents

THE WRONG

CARMEN CAMBRIDGE

"If you couldn't be loved, the next best thing was to be left alone."
~ L.M. Montgomery

THE WRONG

1

"I ugly," I mumble as I peek behind two layers of curtains and through the slit my fingers make between the blinds behind them. The morning light glares against my face and drives a sliver of my reflection against the glass. I see small eyes. They are far apart and, to me, look mean. Well, maybe it's the light in my eyes.

With a sigh I let the curtain fall and turn around to face the room that, after being dazed by the sun, looks a lot darker and bluer than it really is. Until I can see right again, I sit still against the arm of the sofa and try not to think too much about the things I can't change. These thoughts make up almost every thought I have. I feel sad all the time. The man gives me vitamin B and tells me not to worry. But I see the worry in his face and neither of us can ignore my ugliness when, between the two of us, so much effort is made to conceal it.

The man is in the adjoining room making breakfast. His shoulder passes in and out of sight. Every once and a while I see him check on me. I remember when, especially when I was little, our eyes couldn't meet without wanting to smile. I made him complete. He made me happy. Today, I don't even know if I *can* smile. There are tears in my eyes. Almost always there are…or the nose tingling, eye stinging threat of them. The man's brow creases. I see concern and love in his face.

"You okay?" he asks me.

I nod.

He leans in on his right foot like he wants to take a step toward me, then relaxes on his heel. When he turns around to check on breakfast, I notice him wipe the back of his finger under one eye. The muscles in his jaw jump. His Adam's apple bobs as he swallows hard. I think I hurt him. He thinks he hurts me. The truth is that we would *never* hurt each other, but someone has to take accountability for the hurt and confusion. We're the only ones here.

"Feel like an omelet?" he asks. I hear plates clinking. The meal's prepared. I agree without so much as a grunt. It's up to him to make sense of the silence. I *felt* agreement. That's all I have energy for.

I can see normally again and get up. The couch complains as I remove my weight. So, I feel worse. One tear escapes by the time I reach the threshold of the kitchen.

The man is still wearing night pants, but the tee and unbuttoned flannel shirt are worn either day or night. He almost always wears layers. His long, bedraggled brown and graying hair obscures the unshaven man as he leans over the frying pan. I see he's put fruit in the omelet. My favorite. He abandons the skillet to hold me. I start to cry uncontrollably. He strokes my head and tells me, "It's okay."

It's okay that I cry?

It's going to be okay?

The man is sparing with words. "Okay" is universal and he relies on it more than any other word. "Fine" is the angry version of "okay". He never uses "fine" to say that's what I'll be.

When the tears are used up, the eggs are cold. The milk and juice are warm. We eat breakfast in silence.

It's my job to do the dishes.

He pushes his chair back and opens the sliding glass door just enough that he can blow out the smoke from the cigarette he's about to light. There is a stain on the door again. I make a mental note to get after it. The stain worries me. It makes me think of where the smoke goes when he breathes it. What color is the man inside?

"How's the rash?" he murmurs around the hand rolled cigarette. He squints when the smoke reaches his eyes. He's putting the paper and tobacco inside his shirt, so he hasn't bothered yet to lean toward the door.

I look down at my legs, but I can't see them through my own pajama pants. So I look at my arms instead. With a soapy plate in one hand, I raise my arm so he can see. He leans in, squinting harder and frowns deeply at what he sees.

"That's it then. We'll hafta stick to razors."

I sigh and return to the breakfast dishes. There's just two of us. It doesn't take long…or it shouldn't. I wash the same glass a couple times. I soak and scrub the man's coffee cup until the brown ring is gone.

I feel his eyes on the back of my head. He's wondering what the sigh meant. I'm disappointed, but I understand. Trying the cream again might make things worse. Obviously my skin doesn't like it. I don't know that it even left me as smooth as the commercial said. Both of us were still recovering from the experiment with waxing. The look of shock and guilt the man wore after that event is stuck in my memory. It helps that it took almost two weeks before he started to forgive himself.

The *first* time I ever saw guilt on his face, he wore it fewer days, but *never* forgave himself. We don't talk about that.

We talk about getting one of those permanent hair shock-away gizmos. Neither of us feels comfortable going through with it. If the man couldn't afford it, he would have just said so.

"'m okay," I assure the man.

His steady gray-green eyes study me for sincerity. Gone are the days of annoyance and frustration at reading each other's mannerisms, expressions and instincts. He reads me like I have a thought bubble. Now, there are times when I wish he couldn't read me so well. He says that's because I'm growing up. Teenagers, apparently, are like that. Not that I know. The man tells me not to confuse TV with reality. People on TV are not like the ones that live around here. They might not be like people anywhere.

"Okay," the man answers.

I hear pain in his voice. I glance over my shoulder as best as I can, but I have to turn my upper body a little to see him. I'm not as flexible as the man.

He's watching me.

Don't hurt, I think at him. All I do is frown with concern.

He finishes his cigarette and gets up. He needs to comb his hair. It could probably use a washing. He casts another worrisome look at me before heading down the hall toward the back of the house. There are three rooms back there. His bedroom. My bedroom. The bathroom. I hear a dresser drawer open and the stiff sound of denim being pulled through a narrow space. He stuffs his drawers too full.

I have a drawer stuffed too full too. It is full of clothes I've asked for, but found I couldn't wear once they got here. The man always offers to send them back, but in my heart I dream of being able to fit in them someday and keep them to remind me. This "reminder" sometimes helps me feel crappy. The man works hard to take care of me, so I don't throw away anything he buys me, even if I can't use it.

The man emerges from his bedroom at almost the same time as the sink drains. I missed a fork. I scrub and rinse it when he's sitting down in his chair again, stuffing his feet into work boots. I think… I think he might have combed his hair. Maybe.

"What are you gonna do today?" he asks me, looking up through a curtain of his hair, bent over, tightening and tying his laces. I suppose he is handsome. He is more handsome, to me, seeing him like this, than when he's got his shoulder length hair under control. I think women find him attractive too. Though, for all the time I've known him, I've been the only female in his life. I don't think he resents me. I think he's made me his whole world. Everything else in the world? We try to work around it and interact with it as little as possible. Our every action outside this house, is governed by fear of the Wrong People.

I gesture to the indoor greenhouse, which is almost completely hidden between the sliding glass door and the blackout curtain.

"Garden," I answer with a shrug. It's been a couple weeks since the last frost. The seedlings are desperate for room to stretch their roots. I want to go outside. The man looks uncertain. One of his most used expressions.

"Okay…" he agrees tentatively. He doesn't bother to remind me to follow the rules. *I'm not* desperate to stretch my roots. I take the rules as seriously as he does.

I can tell by the look on his face that he's going to be anxious all day.

"No worry," I tell him, for what little good it will do.

He nods and nods until it winds down to nothing. Then, his head is drooped, looking between his knees at the floor or his shoes. His lower arms are resting on his thighs. He fidgets with the dry flap of skin where a blister broke on his thumb a few days ago.

Somewhere in his silence, the man either convinced himself it'd be okay or that he simply needed to get going, because he stood abruptly and leaned over the corner of the table to hug me goodbye. I wrap my arms around the man and push my face into his shoulder. I'm about as tall as him now, but it's still easy to remember when he used to carry me around. That was my favorite thing, my head in the crook of his neck. For the longest time I couldn't rest without being there. His hair in my face. His beard or stubble on the side or back of my head. His hands holding me securely. Mine, clinging to him.

"I love you too," he said when we had to let go. Sometimes he'd look back when he left, but most the time he couldn't. I peeked through the curtain and watched until he was in his truck and as far down the driveway as I could before the tan truck was hidden by the dense forest that surrounded the man's land. In all this time, I only saw him look back once. If he looked back, he'd come back.

I hate to see him leave. This was more than just a matter of not looking. I wasn't as good at resisting as the man. I had to imagine what the windows looked like from outside. If someone was in the yard or meadow, could they see me?

I'd never been told what the Wrong People would do if they showed up, but the seriousness of the man's warnings and rules made knots in my gut. I felt dread.

Before I go for our small greenhouse, I wrap a long scarf around my face, neck, and over my head. I put on my hat with the mosquito netting. I roll the greenhouse from behind the curtain. I did good. If someone were trying, I don't think they would have seen me.

Before I leave the front of the house, I lock the sliding door and slip a bar into the track. I lock the front door and double check that everything in the kitchen is shut off. I have to turn off the coffee pot. The "skin" of an omelet lay like yellow lace on the stovetop. I pop it into my mouth and tromp heavily out of the kitchen. My garden shoes and gloves are in the mudroom on the back of the house. The man's hunting and barn clothes are back there too.

The roosters crow at the morning sun. They crow at the noon and afternoon sun too. They crow at night. TV people are wrong about a lot of things. I wish they were right about roosters only crowing in the morning. I was fascinated at first. Then I thought it was funny to hear them crowing in the middle of the night. If you guessed I would find it annoying at some point, you'd be right. Though there is little comparison between their worst crows and the shrill alarms the man's guinea fowl make. This morning he let the speckled beasts out into their run. It's covered in chicken wire and has several dead trees laid out in it for the birds to roost on. None of the animals are allowed to graze freely when the man isn't here.

Well… almost none.

The man's dog is laying on the back step. It's a gray and black speckled mutt with large black splotches. Her chain's reach is generous. She can get to food, water, shade, the back door, the front corner of the house, and close enough to the barn to scare predators. I'm not good with names. I call her dog. She calls me nothing. The man says that names are used to tell us apart. I would know he was there if there were no light and no sound. I don't think, to him, it's that simple, but he doesn't try to make me remember names anymore.

Dog raises her head and idly wags her tail. She means hello and nothing more. I haven't earned anything more. I let myself out the whining screen door and pet her as I pass by. She wags harder then, spinning rather than swinging her tail. Her fur is soft and dense. I wish my hair was so soft.

I wish I could take her off the leash, but that's not allowed unless the man is home.

Between the rows of plants, the man laid out straw paths for me to walk on. It is golden and squeaks and rustles as I cross it. I like the way it feels and smells. Man says it will help stop weeds and keep my feet from sinking in when the dirt is soft. Offhandedly, the man mentions that the straw will make it harder for the Wrong People to see our tracks and I should be careful not to leave any. Most people don't remember the shy toddler who he sometimes brought to town. Man says it's better that way.

I made it halfway through the beans when I was weeding the day before yesterday. Man told me not to go outside yesterday for *any* reason. I wondered why, but I listen to what he says without asking.

My fat fingers are not as good at delicate work as the man's. I've ruined things. He's never blamed me, but I think he must sometimes wish I hadn't gotten so big. I do too.

Only when I've gotten down and been working for a couple hours do I realize that I'm still wearing my pajamas. Gardening gloves, flip-flops, broad-rimmed mosquito netted hat, a pink t-shirt and fleecy pants with cartoon cat heads all over it…I think I must look like some of those weird people that get picked up on *Cops.* Me and the man watch it almost every day. Some people on there we laugh at and we don't even feel bad! I've asked the man many times if the people are real. Every time he replies, "Afraid so." We don't like all the same shows. He doesn't watch *Catfish* with me and I don't watch *In the Heat of the Night* with him.

Dog raises her head. She cranes to one side like she's trying to look around something in her way. With a snarl she soars over all five steps and takes off around the side of the house, howling and barking madly.

I don't even realize I ran, until the porch's screen door slams shut behind me. The "BANG!" startles me and I pitch myself against the wall to get away from the sound. Like a piece of peanut buttered bread I stick to the wall for some time before peeling off. Then, I am almost too scared to move, but I have to get inside the main house. Seconds later, the inner door slips quietly into its frame. The latch slides soundlessly into its slot. From the racket dog is making there wasn't much chance that anyone heard me, but unless or until there was *no* chance, there was no room for taking any.

There is a knock at the door.

My scalp prickles and goes numb. The sensation passes through my arms and thighs. It feels a little like the time man let me try iced tea with a splash of tea flavored vodka.

The morning light hits the front of the house and whoever it is at the door. Through the three small diamond shaped panes of frosted glass on the heavy front door, I see the silhouette of a man. I can smell his body, but mostly soaps or another strong fragrance I don't like very much. Involuntarily I snuff at the male odor and suddenly became very curious about what he looks like. The stranger doesn't knock again. He turns away, his silhouette growing paler and paler, like the frost is growing over it. He goes loudly down the stairs and tells dog to be quiet. A car door shuts, briefly increasing the volume of the music he is already listening to too loudly. Then I hear the vehicle turn around and take off down the long driveway.

I run to the door and look out the peephole the man installed almost a year ago. I manage to identify the stranger as the mailman seconds before he disappears into the wooded length of the driveway. Dog's bark changes. The enemy is running away. "And never come back!" she seemed to say. I want to let dog in the house. Man will bring her in when he gets home. I wish he was home right now.

When I am anxious for him to return, I do a lot of work. When I miss the man *really* bad, I do a lot of laying around.

I don't feel like doing any more work.

I am afraid to go into the three season porch, because so much of it is screened in. It is not a "safe" place. I take off all my work stuff and leave it at the back door. I hear dog's chain on the steps. She's laying back down, but she still growls quietly.

I go to the kitchen for half a dozen hard-boiled eggs to snack on while I'm curled up on the couch. I sit on *my* side, never the man's side. I have to pull up the foot rest by hand because once I yanked the handle too hard and broke it. I hear the couch complain about me again as I flop back into my territory. I drag a blanket from the back of the couch and pile throw pillows around me. I think I look as pathetic and sympathetic as I feel. I think it would be unfair if I didn't.

I don't like the remote. The buttons are too small. The man promises to get me a special one with large buttons for Christmas. Last year I was smaller and didn't bother man with these kinds of stupid problems. For now, I use one of the pieces from a board game to push the buttons. It is shaped like a chocolate kiss, but has a longer point and a nub that's just the right size for depressing the buttons on the remote. I use the yellow piece because it's my favorite.

I watch the people on TV carefully. I have learned not to trust their behaviors or their versions of reality, though I still think there's something to learn from it. I know a lot about what hair is *supposed* to look like when it's pretty and healthy. I know what people are supposed to look like when *they* are those things too. People point out things about each other—both the way other people look and how other people behave. They laugh at some things and want to mate with others. That's how I came to the conclusion that the man is attractive. His body is a lot like the bodies people seem to like to see naked. Before, I didn't see that many TV men with scruffy faces or beards, but now a lot of them look like him that way too. I like it a lot better. I have always liked facial hair on the man. Come to think of it, I don't know that I have ever seen him without it.

To be honest, men without facial hair don't convey maleness to me.

I watch talk shows, court shows and cooking shows. I know 'who the father is' and things you shouldn't say to a judge. I learned the difference between chopping and mincing. I showed the man, so now I have jobs in the kitchen I didn't have before.

I snarf down the eggs and wish I had more. I have no intentions of getting up. I'm watching reruns about teenagers with babies. It makes me sad to watch it, but I can't stop. The wrong day, the wrong mood, and even a coffee commercial can depress me.

Everyone is better than me.

Sometimes I feel like I should have a baby. It's been a little while since the first time the feeling hit me. The man didn't seem surprised by it. Sometimes he's good at anticipating changes in me. Though I think he's a little overwhelmed by my size.

On TV, I watch the people non-TV people want to see. None of them look like me.

I let myself fall asleep when I feel the least bit drowsy. I am awakened by the man's truck when it pulls into the yard. He's halfway up the steps when he hesitates. When he starts walking again, his steps aren't as hurried. I hear the sound of cardboard skimming briefly across the deck as he picks up whatever the mailman left. He makes a little grunting sound when he stoops to collect a letter I hear drop. After the screen door opens, I hear the jingle of keys.

I'm looking over at him when he comes in. I pout and watch him sadly so he knows just how I feel. His eyebrows are already tilted upward in the middle and I know he's worried how I handled the delivery. He sets the parcels in his spot on the couch and comes to sit beside me. He puts one arm behind me and the other pets my face.

"You okay?" he asks me.

I nod against his shoulder.

"You?" I return.

He lets out whatever air's in his lungs. It only makes sound when it passes through his teeth.

"Yeah."

"Food?" I ask next, hunger returning with a vengeance.

"We can have salads," he suggests. I love salads, but he will be hungry in a couple hours. I try to get him

to eat as much as I do, but he says he can't. I don't see
how he can get hungry so fast if he's full from what he
eats.

I suggest baked potatoes. We don't have to eat the
same thing. Half the time I love a compromise.

"I you, you me," I offer. I only feel okay asking
him to make my dinner because fixing a salad is easy.
Lettuce and fruit cocktail. If he does that, then I will do
the harder job and cook for the man. I'm not allowed
to use the stove, but I can make the potatoes and a
vegetable in the microwave. Man will have to make
the meat himself. I don't prefer meat, but the man
certainly does. There are some chicken wings he could
have.

I get up to make food.

When I look at the man, he's pinching between his
eyes. Then his hand flattens out against his forehead
and for a moment he just sits there like that. He's
leaning into the hand. He doesn't care what we eat.
He's got something else on his mind. It makes me wish
I could make the whole meal and take care of him
better. I don't ever want to make him sorry when he
thinks of me. I don't ever want to seem like trouble.

"Mad?" I ask the man.

He looks over at me. I admire the color of his eyes
while he decides how he's going to answer.

"Never."

I want an explanation. I stare at him so he knows it.
It doesn't take long before it's obvious he won't share
what he's thinking or feeling. I sense… helplessness.

Before we even start making dinner, and obviously
still tired from a hard day's work, the man goes out to
check the animals. On his return, the dog is unleashed

and flies through the house like she's just discovered her legs. Her hips swing wide as she reels around the coffee table. There they connect to the corner with a loud "thunk". The force drives the table almost a foot from where it rested. Unfazed, the wriggling creature takes off for her bed, to the right of the hearth, and plows herself through it. She is preoccupied with her odor.

"You're still in pajamas," the man remarks when he joins me in the kitchen. I grin toothily at him and it surprises a smile onto his face.

"You were careful outside?"

"Mm-hmm," I assure him.

"You were covered?"

I look at him, a look verging on disbelief. *Of course!*

Even though it is some time before the anxious months when hunters venture out into the state forests that touch the man's property, he is always concerned about someone passing through and ending up in our back yard—the only place outside where I can go without the man.

"I saw signs of dogs," he mentions offhandedly. In this part of the country, if not in all others, this didn't necessarily signify a person must be present. The problem was the dogs. I don't remember dog not liking me, but the man said he was really afraid for me, back when I was little, about what dog herself would do to me if she was able to get at me. That the man bothered to mention it told me "afraid" didn't cover what he really felt. I knew other dogs didn't like me. *That* was why he mentioned it now. That is why he mentioned it that way.

"Okay," I mutter.

There was no point on harping on the fact that, compared to dogs, I was slow. That even one would be hard enough for me to deal with. Strays tend to form packs, when they run in the wild, the man said. Some of the "domestic" is stripped from them. Some kill for sport. The man would not have mentioned them if he were not afraid they would show up.

The man won't show me how to use guns—but he owns many. Probably more than I know about. Even if he had been willing, I think about my chunky fingers and can't imagine them fitting where he so easily slips his index finger. I'm not defenseless, but close. But the prospect of feral dogs worried me more for dog than for myself. *I* wasn't tied up outside ten to twelve hours a day.

"Eggs?" I look at the bucket in his left hand. I can smell them. And there are always eggs, but I want to know how many.

"Twenty-three today," he tells me.

I'm delighted.

2

The rest of the afternoon goes well until I go to have a shower and get ready to unwind before bed. Before that, we were watching our programs and temporarily distracted from our problems. I can't go into the bathroom without facing them.

There are three mirrors. The large mirror over the sink, the long mirror on the back of the door and mirror on the extending arm, which the man uses for shaving.

People who are beautiful look at themselves a lot. There must be some kind of amazement when they see the gorgeous person in the mirror and have to accept that it *really* is them. Ugly people have an almost identical experience when we look into a mirror. There was a time when I thought no more about my reflection than to just be fascinated by having one. Following that, I liked the way I looked. After *that*... there was no more of that. The man said he was sorry he ever let me see TV.

I think I would have still known I was... wrong.

I throw the bottle of cream hair remover away and relocate my can of shaving cream. I replace the razor, which I'd thrown away, thinking I was done with it forever. The man says a lot of people painstakingly remove all the hair from their body, just like I do. Do they *really* slather themselves in cream, sparing places where they think they should have hair, and shave the rest?

I never want to think the man would lie to me. Lying, he said, is wrong. If you feel like you need to be deceptive, it's better to not speak. There's nothing wrong with silence.

I go through all the steps to leave the normal amount of hair on my repulsive body. Then I rub a cream over myself that is supposed to help with ingrown hairs. I powder my joints and anywhere that, if slightly damp, will make my clothes cling when I dress. I dry my head and wrap the towel around me. The man is having trouble finding me a bra, but he is checking a few places online where he may be able to order custom sizes.

I brush my teeth, which are white and straight, but remind me of the man's horses'. I scrutinize my short, straight lashes. My lips are almost nonexistent. My ears are too small, I think, for my head. I want someone to like this, but *I* can't. I want to be loved like TV people. I want to have a baby… or babies. It's a panicky feeling. It feels desperate, sometimes. I can make no sense of the needs that I've started to have. Since the first time I felt this way, I find that I judge the men on TV a lot more. I even rate them.

The man is free to go out and meet females…does he not have the same needs as I do?

Will there ever be a time when I'm not confused.

In my bedroom, where almost everything is yellow, I put on a little of the perfume the man bought for me "since I'm growing up". One squirt is almost too strong for me to stand, so I carefully depress the cap until just a little liquid comes out. I don't like fake smells. I don't like to mask the smells that are mine. I want to fit in. I don't want to be wrong.

The man always considers me. Beyond just getting me the perfume he chose a fragrance that has a really wide sprayer. He didn't smell it first, but thought "Candy" sounded like something any girl would like.

I put on a 5X robe and men's slippers, but the man promised me no one could tell the difference. It will be chilly in the mornings for a little while. Then it will be too hot for sleeping.

I hear the man making popcorn. I hear the dog's nails pacing between the linoleum in the kitchen and the adjoining hardwood floor. Dog is greedy. Dog also has no mate and, I suppose, must replace one desire for another. She and I are a lot alike, in that way.

I recently asked the man for a baby, like the ones I see in the weekly toy ads. He studied me for a long time after I asked. Then, with a hint of sadness, agreed, unsurprisingly with, "Okay."

I once asked the man, as best I could, about why there was no woman here. With anything important, he takes his time in answering. Looking elsewhere, he replied, "Sometimes when you try something it turns out so bad you never want to try again."

I'm not sure how that answered my question, but I couldn't stop thinking about how reluctant he is to let me quit anything.

Man is coming down the hall. I meet him at the door.

"You okay?" he asks, idly tucking a strand of my hair behind my right ear.

"Yeah," I say, like it's obvious.

I feel his eyes trying to reach into mine. When he cannot find what he's looking for, he tells me that the popcorn is done. *Cops* will be on soon. I'm sick of the routine. Sick of being ugly. Sick of him prying, with careful questions and long hard looks. I'm sick of living this way. I don't want to be outside. I want to run. I feel like I could tear right through the walls. Uproot a tree. I can't find what I want here. I can't find what I need. Why am I here? Why am I here? WHY AM I HERE?

"FINE!!!" I yell into his face.

Man recoils so fast that he hits the opposite side of the hall with force. Dog darts out of sight. She always hides behind the man's rocking recliner.

I can hear the man's heart racing. I can smell the sweat that jumped onto his skin like beads of ice water. His pale eyes are wide with surprise and fear, even as his body assumes perfectly composure, save a tremor in his fingers.

I am ashamed and I'm afraid of being punished. Never, truly, has man punished me harshly… no matter how I felt about it at the time. After the *last* time, I doubt he will ever let himself seem too angry or use as much body language—which is really what set me off.

My emotions are running high. I hope he understands. I hope I will not be punished.

When the neighbor's dog went after me, I wasn't punished for what I did. Man was protective of me, but I smelled fear in him. I think that was when I first realized I could "freely" assert my anger. Though none of it was directed toward him, I felt and saw weakness in the man in the wake of an emboldened me. Pursuit of dominance feels natural in me. As natural as feeling the need to claim everything that's mine as mine and staking out territory. My bedroom. My toiletries. *My* side of the couch. My patch of mushrooms. My pencil. My fork.

The last time I lashed out at the man, he was firm with me. He asked, "Are you done?" Like I was having a tantrum. I heard the almost inaudible tremble in his voice. In fact, he gave away everything but strongest sign of being afraid—he did not run.

Afterward, I was afraid of what would have happened if he had.

Instead of, "Are you done?" in a calm, caring voice, the man asks if there is something bothering me. After that, when I don't answer, he wants to know, "Were you inside when the mailman came?"

There is tension in his voice. He is worried. I don't blame him. Aside from the animals, I am his whole world. I don't know much, but on TV people don't like to be alone. He has no mate. I'm the closest thing he has to offspring. People are social creatures. I haven't been around people for a long, long time and I am lonely. How lonely is the man? One cannot find true happiness when you live for your responsibilities. I am not just a responsibility, but sometimes I don't feel like I count…no more than dog. People rely a lot on words to communicate. I'm not good at talking. The man has to accommodate me. I guess it's good he's not one for talking much. I am not surprised that he should try to overlook my outburst and blame it on fear of the stranger. It is suddenly clear as crystal, he is afraid to deal with my anger.

"What came?" I change the subject for both of our sake. I don't want him to be afraid of me. I don't want him to decide he can't handle me. What would happen then? The man is sincere when he says meeting the Wrong People would be the worst thing that could happen. Not everyone is as nice as he is, he said. I could tell he meant it. Even before I understood the words he used, I understood what he felt when he spoke them. It terrified me.

When I was very little, he took me into the place called "town". I vaguely remember it and do not trust these memories as honest reflections or figments drawn from TV. He couldn't leave me alone back then. I remember the deeply hooded coat I wore. I remember his smell as I linked my arms around his neck. At first I smelled and smelled to make sense of it—then I bonded with the smell of man. It became the smell of safety. Of home. Of my kind…even though no one looks anything like me.

I follow him to the living room, fixated on his straight backed gait. I am so big that I hunch a little. I think that the weight of my upper body pulls me down. This seems especially true in my low, rounded shoulders.

Then the man calls back, his voice straining to sound nonchalant, even playful, "You must be wondering if it's for you."

That's too easy. The man almost never gets any of the boxes from the mail people. I rack my brain for anything I've asked for. Sometimes he says we can't have something and then surprises me with it. The man seemed a little embarrassed about looking at bras. He explained how I could get the measurements myself. I knew he had some ideas which stores might be able to get the size I need. It could be a bra… or bras. Maybe some pretty lacy underthings. When we were looking at the catalogue, I oohed and ahhed at them, and with special pleasure and interest in the ones I really wanted.

I'm guessing on the inside and want to offer my predictions to the man, but I don't want to ruin the surprise by being right…or make him feel bad if I venture a guess, with a little extra hopefulness, and that is not what he bought for me.

Ninety-percent of the man' body is focused on the package. His left hand steals away and deftly turns on the driveway alert. He is so quick and silent that I barely catch him doing it. I am bothered that he does this—not him being sneaky, but that he turns on the alarm. Getting the device seemed like a good idea at first, but we were nervous wrecks from all the dinging and donging that went on because of deer and critters tripping the motion sensor.

I bet the gun comes off the wall tonight…

Over the fireplace there is a long, fine rifle. It has a large scope, but there is actually a larger scope in the box on the mantle to its left. To the right is an identical metal box and it holds ammo. The man owns many guns…a twenty-two by the back door for varmints. A couple shotguns. A number of other rifles, some of them very, very old, he said. There is the sleek black Beretta in the hidden place by the bed. And the strange looking gun, he never named to me, which has a long curved clip like a banana. That gun and a pair of handguns are in a locked and lighted glass display on the man's wall. There are patches and pins in there too. There are some foreign objects, mostly metal, that the man called shrapnel.

I saw that rifle come off the mantle twice, ever. Once because of the big brown bear that went after the pigs. The other time, he sat up with it all night and a day—the driveway alarm on, sitting up in a stiff-backed chair, or pacing and peeking out curtains, smoking up the cigarettes like people chow down on chips.

What happened that day?

Did someone in town ask about me?

Were there Wrong People around?

"Never mind about that," the man sees right through me. He nods once at the alarm and tells me he's just in a weird mood today. A little jumpy, he says. I can't tell if he's lying. It is probably a half truth.

He presents the package to me and I let my worries fly away. The man always takes care of me. He will always take care of me. Only when he is gone can I justify worry, but even if something happened, I know he would deal with it. I don't know what I am afraid will happen. I never know. The man is vague, I think because the answer is horrible.

I "Ooh!" with pleasure and greedily accept the disappointingly light box. I ban it from showing in my face, but it feels like an empty box. I wonder if bras are light.

"Push bra?" I can't help but ask. The man frowns deeply, almost scowls. He firmly asserts a "No".

I whine.

"Absolutely not," he shakes his head. "*Eck!* No."

"Eck?"

"Yes, 'eck'. You are way too young… You'll always be too young."

I smile, enjoying the bantering. I can't help but laugh, even though, when I think of what they do and how bad I need it, I really want that kind of bra.

I take the box to the open floor between the coffee table and the entertainment stand. This is the most open floor space in the living room and I like to sit on the rug. There used to be a fur one here, but the man took it away when I started to really get around on my own.

The papery tape crinkles and draws the dog out of her hiding spot. She sniffs the air for the smoky scent of most her treats. She is disappointed and goes to the man to mooch for a treat. He tells her if I am getting a treat, she may have one. Dog likes provolone and gets a slice. It has smoked flavoring—surprising no one that she loves it.

I cannot believe my eyes when I fold back the first and second sets of flaps. I clamp a hand over my mouth and feel a tremor of joy become the stinging of tears. I throw a look of disbelief at the man and a broad smile sweeps the exhaustion and worry from his face. He is pleased with himself. I think this is why he buys nothing, or very little, for himself. My joy is his joy.

"On?" I barely manage to say.

"Please," the man says. His eyes look especially sparkly.

Getting up is awkward. Readily, I blame my size. The man says it has to do with my bones… big bones, he probably means. This depreciating thinking lasts only until I am standing. I run for my bedroom. On either side of me I hear things begin to shake. The antler and fake candle chandelier in the living room dances on its chain. The man steadies a lamp. Anything that can clink is clinking in the cupboards, pantry, closets and shelving. I only hear one thing fall. As I burst into my bedroom, I see it hit the floor—my favorite plush—a little monkey. I remember when I was small enough that it filled my arms. Now it is fit for little more than my hand and stirring pleasant memories from the shelf over my bed.

Considerately, the man has moved over by the fireplace. There he cannot see me until I am ready, ruining nothing of the surprise. I love him for this and the way he looks at me when I walk in.

"Oh my...Oh sweetheart, you look beautiful."

I *feel* beautiful and stroke the shoulder length wig, clearly flattering what is most difficult to help, my face. I feel lovely. I feel desirable. I feel like tearing off my clothes and rampaging through the woods. I feel bestial. My heart soars.

"Bring man," I say. My heart is pounding so hard I can hardly think.

The joy flickers on the man's face. He takes a second more to *really hear* what I said. Then the joy dies out entirely. He looks helpless and serious. He is struggling for words. He may be struggling for a thought he can do something with. I grow impatient. Is he just trying to think of a nice way to say something mean?

"I can't do that," he says steadily. He wants me to hear and understand every word.

"Want!" I cry.

He sighs.

What does he want to say? 'I can't get you everything you want' or maybe, 'I could never do *that* to someone'.

I feel my body changing, responding, both in rage and embracing how pretty I feel—I feel ready to meet men. I *feel* ready. So ready—I feel like screaming, clawing, pawing, biting—CRUSHING!!

He thinks I am spoiled. He thinks I'm a brat. No good now. Now that I am grown or growing, having a female around is uncomfortable. It's no wonder then, is it? IS IT?!—that he should be living out here, in the middle of nowhere. Alone. If no woman would love him—why should *I* love him?

"I wish I knew there was someone for you—like… you… People aren't like dolls. Fake people can be bought. Fake people can be brought home. Real people can't."

I roar at him.

"Shh—SHH!" and severely, I think, he says, "STOP."

I feel like he's going to hit me. I take a step back.

He's shushing me, one raised finger tapping against his lips. He's looking at the windows, there is nothing to see. There is never anything to see. What is the point of looking? The curtains keep out everything, even sunlight.

Is there really anything to fear? Am I really as ugly as TV makes me feel? He said real life and TV are not the same. I want to feel comfortable in my skin. Am I maybe so beautiful that he is afraid of men seeing me? Has the man always wanted to keep me to himself all this time?

I don't think I will shave anymore...

I want to have long hair like all the pretty TV women.

"You *can't* be loud like that!" he snaps at me. He does not know how lucky he is to be on the other side of the room. "Sound is not stopped by these walls!" He drives the soft side of a fist against the log wall. "When you're out in the barn, you hear the wind chimes in the front yard. You hear the phone ring. Inside, you hear the roosters crow and, when the nights are hot and you open your window a crack—you hear the calls of distant animals—*distant* animals."

His chest is heaving with fear, alarm, anger, frustration. His gray-green eyes blaze, as they only do when he's upset.

"I love your squall," he says more gently. "I remember the first time you did it—I was shocked, but I was amazed by you. Sweetheart, its unique...that means no one is going to hear it and think it is something else. They will never believe anything they try to think it is. I know you want to do it—the way the rooster wants to crow—but you must never do it again. Do you hear me? Nobody can ever know about you."

I'm not surprised he'd say that...especially not now. Now that I have the wig. I will probably never get the bra...especially not the kind I want. I nod, but I feel smug and defiant. I do not feel the affirmation I give. I do not yet know how long I'm going to feign compliance.

Sometimes he makes me feel like a captive. Some people feel more comfortable caged. They like to be limited. Simplicity. Safety. Though the man goes out, works, and likes outdoor activities like hunting, fishing, hiking, farming—he is held captive by wanting so much privacy. He shrinks away from social interaction. He's a hermit, in some ways. I used to blame myself that he rushed home because of me. That he refused to meet co-workers after work or other occasions because he didn't want to leave me by myself. This is not my fault. This is his choice. He's not going to make me feel bad about it anymore.

The man watches me intently, trying to read me. He is about to say something when the alarm beeps three times. I am surprised that the man does not hurry to the door, instead he takes out a device I have never seen before. It looks something like his phone and phones I've seen on TV, but it is not *his* phone…as far as I know.

He taps the screen and does nothing for several seconds. He is not checking messages or sending any. He has not answered the phone. He does nothing because something is happening on the screen.

"What that?" I want to know.

His eyes look pale and very gray when they move off the screen and over to me.

"Come over," he encourages me and I go. It seems he has forgiven me, or forgotten the matter, for the moment.

When I am shoulder to shoulder with him, actually I think I am slightly taller, he turns the screen to me. I watch a black and white video of a heavily wooded forest and a long dirt driveway running through it. There is a fine mist hanging in the air. It fades away before my eyes.

"What *that*?" I press him.

"Dirt," he says.

I raise an eyebrow and he allows a half smile.

"I know. It's strange. It's like the chicken's dusting. That cloud is really fine dirt."

"Chick?" I point at the screen.

"No," he answered somberly. "A vehicle did that."

The other eyebrow rises to the height of the first.

The man puts a hand on my back and rubs it gently.

"I need to go deal with it."

"Who?" I worry. Wrong People?

"Neighbor," he answers with so little energy that it sounds like the words are being dragged over gravel.

"Gun?" I gesture to the rifle.

"No."

"Not now?" I'm guessing.

He looks stern while he puts away the new device and leaves to put on a jacket.

"No dogs came by when you were out?" he asks nonchalantly. His boots make loud thunking sounds as he stuffs his feet into them. His long hair falls over his face. I'm not sure if he just said something else. I am listening to the sound of a vehicle getting close.

"No," I say.

He has not forgotten the trouble over the dog that came over before. He is, in fact, thinking about it right now. Other than deliveries, I know the man gives no one any reason to stop by.

I hear a door shut. From the volume, the weight of the impact, it is a truck. Man has a truck. Delivery trucks sound different, their doors slide open and closed. Cars make small, dull thuds.

Man is a fine hunter. He is slender, wiry, and alarmingly fast and agile. The strength of his grip is surprising and assuring. Man drives a truck. So is the driver of this foreign truck a similar kind of person? Do they have to be? Are they dangerous too?

The man gets outside before the other person, also a man, reaches the steps.

"Hey, Charlie," I hear the man say to the stranger.

The stranger greets him too.

"Sorry, I know it's late and I hate to bother you, but the missus asked me to stop at all the neighbors' and see if Dottie has shown up at their place."

"Dottie?" I hear the man say.

My skin feels tight. My chest hurts. My heart is jumping like a frog in cupped hands. My legs feel weak. I tremble. I wish the man had brought a weapon. Almost always, he carries something. But the visit was unexpected—I assume—and we were just about to sit down and watch our show. Knife or gun were probably already put down for the night.

"The missus' cat. Got a bur in its ass today, figuratively, and decided it was an outdoor cat. Tore off when she went to hang the laundry. I suspect she stepped on it, but she insists the fur-ball just bolted for no reason."

"What does she look like?" asks the man.

"She's mostly orange fur, but her belly up to her throat is white. I think there might be a little white on one ear. Creepy orange eyes too, if you don't mind me sayin' so."

The stranger has a local accent, unlike the man who, to me, has none. I have a hard time understanding some very strong accents, so I'm thankful this man just shapes his words funny and only skips letters here and there. Sometimes I think people add letters when their accent is really strong. I wonder if the description is of the stranger's wife or the cat. It would be nice to see a hairy woman outside the man's vintage circus cabinet card collection. There are pictures of some strange and, sometimes, scary looking people. None of them are covered in orange fur, but between myself and a few of those people on the cards, nothing would surprise me.

"Cat's not fixed then?"

"Naw," the stranger makes the word last seconds. "The missus can't get enough kittens. She mighta just ran off to meet an old tom, but that cat would look like a nice meal to almost every predator we have around here."

I imagine the man nodding before he answers, "That's true enough. Well w—I'll keep an eye out for her. I'm not using any of my live traps right now. I'll set out a few and see if we don't get lucky. Might be that she'll see the place and, after getting all the way through those woods, will just be glad to see signs of people. I can spare a few cans of Shasta's wet dog food to bait the traps. 'Least she'll be safe and fed until I get a chance to check them."

"That's mighty neighborly, friend," says the stranger.

"That's what we are, Charlie," the man dismisses. Through these words I hear the man smiling. To me, the friendliness in his voice sounds strained. The stranger doesn't notice, but he doesn't know the man as well as I do.

"Well I have just a couple more stops to make. The missus told me she looked online at how far a cat might wander just to mate. So that's the radius I have to piss through to get this errand done. Glad that still don't mean a lot of stops. Not too many folks out in these parts," the stranger says with a laugh. It reminds me of the horses. I hear the stranger walk across the porch to the steps.

"Give my best to Grace," the man opens the screen door. I imagine him raising one hand to say goodbye. He is a stationary waver. I wave with both arms.

"I sure will," the stranger calls from farther away.

Only when the truck is out of sight does the man slip back inside. The door is locked, the porch light off. He reminds me the alarm will go off again when the stranger leaves. We wait tensely for the alert to tell us he is gone and that he did not take too long in going either. *That* really bothers the man.

After the alert is over, we finally sit down to our show—there are always several episodes in a row. The dog is sitting by the coffee table trembling, eyeballing the popcorn bowl with something like love and lunacy. The fur under her eyes is wet.

"Sorry, baby," the man pets the dog and puts a fistful of popcorn on the rug. Because he forgot to take them off when he came in, the man pries his boots off and pushes them under the coffee table with his socked feet. He puts an arm on the back of the couch and looks over at me. I forget that I am feeling belligerent and lean into it. I feel bad that I am getting so big. I am afraid that soon I will be so big that I will hurt him.

I think someday I will.

3

Outside, through my bedroom walls, I hear the night creatures calling each other. I am waiting for one to call me. There are sounds in the dark the man has never explained. I know the sounds of moose, wolves, fox, and night birds. Every once and a while, I will lean up on one elbow and listen so hard that my ears start to ring… It has even brought on headaches. There are whooping sounds, howling sounds, yowling sounds—some, even like barking. Always they are far, far off. I cannot tell how far. Somehow, the man knows, with some certainty, how close or distant an animal is when they call. In the winter, when the wolves drive deer out of the woods and across the frozen lakes, their howls carry eerily through the night air. I guess which lake and the man will say another, in a completely different direction. He asks me to listen harder and when I do I can tell he is right. The man does not have to try. Some things people are born with. Nature, he mastered by experience. He is not a young man. We celebrated his forty-sixth birthday last year. Should I be jealous that he knows more than me? No. I am jealous that there are things only he can answer, but he chooses not to.

I have heard a strange thing tonight—the same strange sound I've heard only a few times before. For a few days in the spring and fall, I hear pounding or knocking in the woods. Maybe wood on wood, or rock on wood, or rock on rock, but almost definitely one combination of these. I can distinguish the sounds, but with something deeper than senses I *know* what it is, but cannot translate it to my mind. How often, when I was smaller, did I reach up under the curtain to open the window and listen to it? I can almost hear the whisper of the fabric against the side of my head as I pressed my ear as near the screen as I could. The sound stirred me. I woke the man several times, unable to resist the urge to beat on the window sill. The man never objected to my waking him to do this. The first time, I remember, I was only waist high on the man. So when he stood beside the bed, I was only a little shorter than him. He held onto me and listened too. He said, "You hear something?" and I nodded my head emphatically. "Yeah?" he said, in the same way he answered questions about Santa or the Easter Bunny. And then, more seriously he'd ask, "What do you think it was?" I'd shrug. He'd hug me and remind me I needed my sleep. That's pretty much how it went the first few times. The last few times, he just asked if I was okay.

Eventually I asked for and was given a drum. Whatever makes the sounds does not seem interested in the sounds it makes, but I get a lot of pleasure from beating on it—I get a lot of comfort…

I rest my chin on the window sill. A trace of sweet night air leaks through the blackout curtains. I smell the greening yard. Over the smell of evergreens is the sweet fragrance of maple and poplar trees budding. What I would give to strip naked and lay out in a fern or cedar bed! My actual bed creaks with the slightest movement. The man has reinforced it, there are heavy L-bars that will hopefully support all the growing I have left in me.

I am too heavy for the bathroom scale. The man thinks I weigh as much as four-hundred-and-fifty-pounds.

Tomorrow I will ask the man to move my mattress to the floor and get rid of the frame. Right now I'd rather sleep on a rug. It doesn't feel right to sleep so high up.

I dream of males. Something is *wrong* with the ones in my dream, but whatever it is does not stay with me outside sleep. I feel confused when I wake up. I know I should feel afraid of what I saw in the dream, but I'm not.

4

I am not roused by the sound of breakfast, but of the man moving through the house, already in his boots. He never lets me sleep in, because he wants me to know when he has left, so I don't worry. And to make sure I remember the rules for when he is away.

I wonder if he is so bothered by our confrontation last night that he is refusing to interact with me now. The cold shoulder... silent treatment... things that happen on TV, not in real life. I don't know if I should stay in my room or try to make it impossible for him to avoid me.

Would he really leave without saying anything to me?

I hear him head back to the kitchen. He's not even trying to walk quietly. I guess he doesn't care if I'm sleeping.

When I leave the room, I am ready for a blow up.

I find the man stooped over the kitchen table, stealing a last minute sip from a nearly full coffee cup. I can smell that it's leftover from yesterday's pot.

"Good morning, sweetie," he says almost before I reach the kitchen.

I suddenly notice how many lights are on. Outside, it is barely the gray of morning. He already has his coat on. There is a little color in his cheeks, a little sweat on his brow. I can smell that he went to the barn already and didn't shower before dressing for work.

"What?!" I inquire.

"Sorry, sweetheart, I was just about to wake you. I got called in."

"Trouble?"

He nods as he eases past me. I am too stunned to give him room. The man excuses himself.

"I'll be back soon, angel. I will call if I know I will be too late, but don't expect me to be on time. If I'm late, I'll need you to take care of the animals…"

I agree. I sound as dazed as I feel.

"That's my good girl," he says. The locks are opened and, now, so is the door.

"Call," I remind him.

"I promise," replies the man.

He runs to his truck. No lunch. No breakfast. He scares a rabbit out from under it when he turns over the engine. I close the door behind him—something I never have to do. Then I watch the headlights disappear down the driveway. Both of us are breaking tradition.

5

It's dark out. I don't like being in the house by myself. I decide to let the dog in. I think the man will understand. If he is still gone when it gets dark tonight, then even if the man is bothered, I won't care that I broke the rules. I will need to have the dog inside.

I notice that the man had started to leave a note for me, beside three packets of strawberry oatmeal—which I love. I eat a couple hard-boiled eggs while I wait for my breakfast to finish cooking in the microwave. I share two yokes with the dog, who looks excited to be inside.

BOOM!

Dog and I howl. I throw myself to the floor. Dog is in her hiding spot. I feel for an injury. I listen for movement. Did I hear someone open the screen door on the back porch? Did the latch just release on the door? I hear the sound of whispers. Then clearly, do I hear the sound of feet, too small and too many to be adults or even people. I heard the screen door open again and again.

BAM!

The lights flickered.

I cower under my arms.

After the crash, I hear something growl overhead. The things I heard walking through the house begin to run!

Whatever was going to happen was going to happen any second.

BEE-BEE-BEE... BEE-BEE-BEE... BEE-BEE-BEE

My oatmeal! It will draw them to me.

But under the roar of tiny feet, I hear the whir of the microwave running.

BEE-BEE-BEE... BEE-BEE-BEE... BEE-BEE-BEE

The phone!

"Man!" I wail into the receiver. My knees knock together. I am vaguely aware of my dash for the phone, but the teetering lamp and overturned kitchen chair mark my path.

"Hi sweetheart," I barely hear him say through the noise on his end. It sounds like static, but it isn't on the phone, it is with him.

"Hiii…" I say weepily. Trembling.

"Just wanted to check on you. If the storm scares you too bad, head down to the cellar. Don't worry about Shasta, she can go under the porch. There are snacks and flashlights down there…and nothing scary. Okay?"

I nod against the receiver. After a little while I give an "mm-hmm".

"See how many episodes of *Gilligan* you can watch before I get home."

"Okay," I say.

"I have to go. Be a good girl."

"Okay," I repeat. I am too scared to digest a lot of what he said. I see flashing lights outside the frosted front door glass. I distinguish the rain from what I thought were small footsteps, but am not comforted. I hate storms.

We say goodbye. I hear the line go dead.

I make sure all the locks are locked. I peek through the peep-hole and see nothing. What light the dawn was fighting to provide was snuffed out by rainclouds too dense or too great to distinguish in torrent blackness outdoors.

I am hesitant, but flip on the porch light.

The light catches every droplet in the downpour, but everything else is hard to see. I think I see something run around the side of the house!

Is the back door locked?

Though I know the pit-pattering is rain on the roof, I am still afraid to enter the hall. All bathroom and bedroom doors are standing open. Those rooms are filled to the doorframes in blackness. I don't have time to be afraid if I am to reach the back door before someone running that fast. When I reach it, I can't decide if I should step out onto the porch to lock the screen door too.

I won't feel safe if I don't.

The back door is partially locked—one dead bolt and the lock on the door are secured. A second deadbolt, floor and ceiling bolt and chain are not locked.

Dog starts barking when I open the back door. She is howling and barking when she comes whipping out of the living room. I think someone is coming up behind me as I step out onto the porch! Instead I am faced with someone on the other side of the screen door, I've just walked through.

I push the door open hard, spilling the person out onto the floor of the enclosed porch. I glance to my right and see the porch's screen door swinging freely on its hinges. In the mere seconds I stand there it bangs against its frame twice, caught in the shifting gusts.

I seize the man by his coat and lift him easily with one hand. From somewhere inside him, something falls heavily to the ground. I look down just in time to see a wooden stand and pole settle to the ground. I smell the man, *my* man, on the stranger—what is left of him. Only then do I realize that I am holding the man's raincoat.

Too afraid to be relieved, I yank the screen door closed, lock it and pitch myself into the house. I secure all of the locks behind me. I pick the dog up in my arms and hug her trembling body. Along her whole back is a hand's width ridge of standing fur. We both need—*deserve* a treat.

We eat the last of the hard-boiled eggs. I reheat my oatmeal and make it too thick and dry. I put jelly on it and then I eat it. I collect snacks for both of us and stock the coffee table with supplies. All the blankets come off my bed. The spare blankets come out of the hall closet. I raise the footrests on both sides of the sofa and put an ottoman in between them. I pile all the blankets on top. Then dog and I start watching the man's collection of the TV show.

There is one disc missing from the collection, and it has been gone since the first time the man and I watched the show together. There is an episode with a monkey. It is old and toothless, as I recall. I was struck by it and had a hard time, emotionally, getting past what I felt when I saw it.

If something hurts me, it always goes away. And always, I assume, it is the man's doing. Though he rarely makes a point of letting me know, unless it will comfort me more to see the thing disappear.

6

On TV, there seem to be no jobs that do not have shows about them or characters who do them. I do not see the man's work on TV. The closest, I think, is the guy who's always chasing the bear who steals picnic baskets. And still, I don't think that's close at all. I think that the man blocks channels where they show his work. I can think of lots of reasons why he might do that. If his work would scare me or make me angry at him, that might be the two biggest reasons. I cannot watch animal channels, discovery channels, science and history channels, among several others. He even blocks some of the public broadcasted channels. Maybe he is *too* considerate. Or maybe he is too *controlling*.

The man is a game warden. I know what a game is. I know what a warden is, from prison shows. He does not dress like the people in games, whose job seems to match "game warden". They call themselves referees. Are they the same thing?

The man does not get special calls very often. He does not tell me what they are about. "Trouble" and "Probably nothing" are the only things he's ever said about the calls. Sometimes I think *he* thinks I can't handle more of an explanation. Whether he thinks it's better if I don't know or if he thinks I am too dumb to understand it, I may *never* know. I have assumed both. In fact, I usually do.

I cannot say all the words I know. Some of the words I feel do not *have* words, that I know of. I cannot talk well. And I am smarter than I sound when I do talk. Nothing comes out as clear as I understand it. On TV sometimes, people treat people like they are dumb just because they don't speak their language well or at all. The person may be a genius and just can't articulate their thoughts in the other person's language. They get treated like children when they are not.

I sympathize with them. I *empathize*.

Naivety and ignorance are not the same as stupidity—the man told me that himself. "Dumb" I'd called myself, when I kept making mistakes in a board game. The first thing the man wanted to know was where I heard that word—TV, of course. And then, after telling me how simple the mistakes were, reminded me that I was just a beginner. I often suspect the man of hypocrisy in matters like that. I wonder if I will ever catch him doing it.

The storm got worse before it got better. For some time the lightning was so constant, it was like the darkness and the lightning traded jobs. During that, the lights went out. There are flashlights all over, but I was too afraid to leave the couch. Were I not afraid of storms, I would have had no trouble reaching them. If the constant, pulsing illumination breeched more than just the frosted glass in the door and, ever so sneakily shone around the edges of the windows, I would have had plenty of light.

Dog and I have finished almost everything on the table. The dog has went to drink several times, but I don't want to leave the covers. I have to make water, but I'd rather stay on the couch. I am ignoring the fact that I am supposed to check on the animals soon. If the man were to come home right now, I would have plenty of time to jump up and pretend that I was just about to do it. Then he would do it.

Dog has been whimpering. She finished her water an hour ago. She scratches at the door for the umpteenth time.

"No," I say to her. I hate the sound of my voice. I begin to flip through the channels. I am looking for nothing in particular. The first thing that grabs my attention will hopefully distract me from the dog.

I feel a wet nose on my wrist.

When I look down at the dog, I do not see it, but my bare skin. I see the hair growing in. I hear the man saying that it looks like I will have to shave soon. I hear my voice, big, low, slow… like drunks on TV. Most of the time I try to make it high, but I don't have it in me. I'm not that successful at it anyway.

Dog bats at my knee through the blanket. I feel the bite of her nails through the cloth—the blankets have slid off my right leg and exposed it. It hurts a little and surprises me a lot. I yowl at the dog and cry, "DOWN!"

I smack her nose and she lets out a yip. She has to pass me to reach her hiding place, so she runs to the kitchen instead, leaving a thin trail of urine most the distance. Under the table, she lets out the rest. She is shitting at the same time.

"NO!"

I hurl myself off the couch and thunder into the kitchen. I raise a hand to punish her, when I see blood running out of her nose and mouth onto the floor. The bridge of her nose is bent down. Her tongue is pinned between two rows of teeth. The top row is wedged behind the bottom row. At my raised hand she tries to get away. I am scared too! What will the man do?!

I catch her by one leg and yank her toward me. There is a popping sound and her back leg flips up like a wing. She is crying and flopping like a fish on a line. I pull her close and try to calm her. The ridge on her back is up. Her eyes are bulging. There is a lot of white and it looks like red cracks are running through it.

I put her under one arm and run to the bathroom. I yank the cabinet door open and off its top hinge. I grab at a towel, any towel, and pull it out. Almost every towel in the three stacks spill out. I wrap the dog's bloody mug and wish it better. The dog struggles. It hurts to be held, but she wouldn't let me help her otherwise. She scratches the tops of my thighs and I forgive her. I don't care. Scratch all you want. And finally, she relaxes across my thighs.

I had a bloody nose once and the man held a tissue to it for what seemed like forever. That was how long I waited before checking the bleeding. The least bit looked like a lot. How could I know if all that blood was *too* much? At least, it looked like the bleeding stopped.

I pinched the end of her mug and tried to separate it from her jaw.

"Good girl," I said, though I felt her stiffen, she did not so much as whimper.

I heard something crunching in the length of her nose. The sound it made, when I straightened it, was like cracking a melon rind. I removed her tongue from the lower teeth and blotted it with a fresh towel. It didn't look like it was bleeding any more either. I would know better when I got her washed up. After all this, she didn't deserve a full bath, which she hates. So I just washed her face. The dog was still afraid. Her eyes, all bloodshot and bulgy, would not face me.

I better get her back outside, I think. If I clean up, there will be no evidence that I accidently hurt dog. For all man knew, the Wrong People came by. For all I knew, this was something they would do.

"Sorry. Sorry," I say as I lift her into my arms. Moving hurts her. She is tense and braced against jarring. I am as careful as I can be.

At the back door, I slip on my flip-flops and unlock everything. I have no trouble holding the dog in one arm. I only hope it doesn't hurt to be held that way.

I pick up her leash from the steps, outside, where I left it. The edges of the wooden stairs are rounded from her trips up and down them with that chain. I open the large door, for accessing the space under the porch. Dog's smaller door is part of it. Underneath, I feel the unwashed air, trapped and stale compared to the fresh cool air outside. No wonder dog prefers to lay on the steps.

I carry her to her dog bed—the top of an old trunk that the man has lined with worn out blankets. When I lay her down, she is still so scared that she is afraid to move in front of me. Two of her legs are raised in a way I think will be uncomfortable for her really soon. She doesn't blink. She will be just fine when she relaxes.

I put her collar back on and pet her. I can't stay and love her up longer, because the man could come home at any time.

I return to the space under the porch to bury the bloody towels and rags I used for cleaning. I know it's not the best choice, but I am not allowed to use the fireplace. I don't have a lot of time to plan anything better. I consider the woodstove, but the man has not used it for several nights, since the weather is getting warmer. This will just have to do, until I can dig them up and hide them better.

I use toilet paper to clean up the pee, because I can flush that down the toilet. I do the best I can on the rug. Then I open a can of cola and pour it where I cleaned. I clean that up. The result isn't great, but that's okay. Now, it just looks like I spilled a drink.

Okay. Okay. She peed here. Bled under there. Then we went to the bathroom.

I stand amongst the towels and am beside myself with helplessness. I am no good at folding towels, never have been. What do I do?

B-EEENG! B-EENG! B-EENG!

The driveway alert!

I scoop up the towels in my arm and cram them on their shelf. I carefully prop up the cabinet door and, with the magnetic latch in place, it holds the door mostly upright. The power *had* gone out. I could have been in the bathroom and bumped into it.

The towels were easy to explain.

Oh no!

I run to the living room. I hear things falling in the other rooms. I hear the cabinet door fall loose. I snatch the kitchen garbage and sweep the evidence of me and dog's meals into it. I unfurl several feet of paper towels and ball up several of these sections into the garbage can to cover the food. I toss the garbage can back where it belongs and thank my stars that it does not tip. Then I am back collecting the blankets and running them to my room. When man brings dog in tonight, I will lay them out on my floor for dog to lay on. Then the man won't think anything of having to launder them tomorrow.

Am I forgetting anything?

I hear the man unlock the door. The door stops fast when he pushes it open. Then the man closes it most the way and calls for me.

"Will you get the chain?" he asks me.

"Oh!" I exclaim and run to be helpful. I open the lock and smile hugely at him. He is sopping wet from rain and sweat and smells like he has been around animals. This has never bothered me. I hug him and draw the smell deep into my nose…into my being.

"Fo'give you," I tell him.

"You forgive me?" he returns, half hugging me, but mostly patting my back. He is tired. I can hear it in his voice. But he also sounds interested, like he doesn't know what I'm forgiving him for. I don't like that.

"Yah," I say, nodding.

"I'm glad," says the man. He doesn't know what for. I can tell.

"You wa' bad," I remind him. After such a long day at work, he deserves a little nudge, if that's what's making him forget.

The man is taking off his coat. His eyes are on me. Even as he stoops over to remove his boots—through the brown hair fallen across his face, ink black with rain and sweat—I see his pale eyes fixed on me. His face says nothing. He is thinking, but he is not trying to remember.

When he stands upright I see his eyes, like a hangnail on linen, briefly catch on the empty water bowl. Then he is walking past me, peeling off layers of wet clothes. When he passes, he watches me. He doesn't walk all the way into the bathroom to toss his shirts into the bathtub. He peels off his socks. I hear them splat against the porcelain. He undoes his belt and heads back to the bedroom. I hear the sound of the regular things being emptied from his pockets. I hear the whisper of his belt slipping through the rings on his jeans.

"Wan' me wo'k barn?"

The man glances at his wrist, where one of the few dried places on his body was already drawing moisture. At the same moment, small amounts of water were gathering underneath the watch, where he just sat it, on the nightstand.

"What time *is* it?" he asked me.

"Late," I say. This answer does not mean nothing. It means that it is later than when he usually comes home, but not so late that he had to call. He has a pretty good idea what that time is. He is nodding at my answer. He understands.

"No sweetie, I'll go. I'm already soaked."

After he says this, he seems to catch again while he's looking at me. Apparently he's not going to share what he's thinking. And he *is* thinking. I can almost hear the gears grinding. He's thinking hard, in fact. He's fixed, concentrating. Thinking too much, if you ask me.

"Dinner?" I offer.

"Sure, hun. Let's do pizza. It's easiest."

For only one second do I interpret it as, 'Let's do pizza because it's been a long day and it will be less hassle.' Then all I hear is, 'You can manage to make a pizza, right?'

I don't answer.

The man goes outside.

It takes a long time to take care of the animals, but it seems like a very long time tonight. On a farm, there are a lot of incidentals that can make chores take longer. I don't know if the storm did anything the man needs to take care of right away. He might spend longer soothing the horses, who can be easily rattled. Maybe he heard the neighbor's cat whining from a live trap and went to rescue it from the rain... but I don't think the man has sat any traps.

And yet, I fear he has.

7

To keep myself busy, while I'm waiting for the man to return, I set the table. I make sure the numbers on the pizza box are the same on the stove and start preheating. I'm pretty sure I did it right. The pizza will be done and cool enough to eat when he gets back. When I hear him on the porch I will pour two glasses of milk. None of this takes as much time as I hope or as much time as I need to fight the anxiousness. Not too long after I do all the possible dinner preparations, I am left standing by the back door. I fold and unfold my hands. I ring them. Lace and unlace my fingers. I pace. I wonder where he is. I wonder what he's thinking.

If the man is mad, I will tell him that dog attacked me. That I was scared to tell him because I thought he'd be on dog's side. But he won't be. Will he?

Then, from under the porch floor I hear a throaty, gagging sound of surprise.

Only then do I realize that I am whimpering. I am pacing again, fidgeting, fidgeting…worrying.

I hear the door under the porch open. I open the back door only enough to peek outside. In the porchlight, I see the man stagger out into the rain. He moves like he has been running for as long as he can stand. When he stops, he buckles forward. His hands slide from his thighs to his knees. This is all that keeps him from falling. He sways side to side like someone idly searching the ground. His hands fly to his face. He folds over in half. I cannot tell if his hands are over his mouth or his eyes. When he stands straight and his hands fall away, I see his shoulders and diaphragm heaving under his barn coat.

He takes several drunken looking steps, out into the yard, and lowers his head. His hands are on his sides. He looks over his shoulder at the house, I duck out of the way. Through the rain and darkness I could not see his face, even if I had stood there and tried.

I hear the man coming up the back stairs. I run to the kitchen and pour the milk. I hear him set down the milk buckets. He props open the back door and moves them inside. Then he goes back for the eggs. By the time the man is inside and taking off his coat, dinner is ready.

Now the man doesn't look at me at all.

"Smells good," he chokes out, clears his throat, and repeats it in a normal voice.

I sigh with happiness and prance back to the kitchen. The man follows slowly. He must not really like the smell.

I have forgotten to take out the pizza and it has cooked almost twenty-minutes too long. The man takes removes it from the oven and points out that it could be worse… I hope he remembers that. The man cuts the pizza and gives me four pieces. He takes one.

I whimper and shove my chin toward his plate.

"I think I'm just too tired," he explains as he drops into his chair. I slide into mine and start shoving the pieces into my mouth. I slather them with ranch dressing and push them into my mouth without bothering to open it as wide as I should. I do not take my eyes off the man. He cuts his pizza with a fork. I see a tremble in his chin before he eats the piece. His brow is knit. He looks up at the kitchen light. I see that the whites of his eyes are pink. He sniffs hard and swallows harder. Then he cuts another piece.

"How bad was the storm out here?" he asks me. His voice sounds strange. He clears his throat again and keeps swallowing, though he's only taken two bites.

"Gill-gan," I say loud and cheerfully, to show him that I had the best time—that it was a good idea. I hold up all my fingers and close my hands. Then I raise a random number of them. "Saw." I tell him.

"That's impressive," he remarks with little effort— all the effort he seems to have.

I wonder why he doesn't bring dog in, but don't ask. Maybe he already assumes that dog attacked me or maybe he doesn't want me to see that the Wrong People hurt her.

"Good milk!" I exclaim.

The man lowers his fork and studies me. The muscles in his jaw are jumping. His eyes fly around the room and land back on me.

"Did I ever tell you about the day I adopted you?"

I am taken aback. I have asked. He has never told me. 'That's for another time,' he always said. 'Not now.' 'When you're older.' 'Not today.' So I am surprised he would volunteer it now, unless he feels bad about upsetting me.

He doesn't wait for me to respond before he begins explaining:

"Forest department got a call that a hiker went missing. Of course, we all knew that the hiker was a poacher—"

"Why?" I wonder.

"We had good reason, but the most important part of this story is you. Okay?"

I smile hugely. Me!

He swallows hard.

"Well, me and another warden tracked him back a long, long ways into some pretty rough country. He was looking for moose. We'd no sooner found the man's rifle when something screamed behind us. The sound was something like a lynx, but bigger and deeper. It was *mad*.

"The next thing I knew, my friend is flying between the tree trunks. I thought I saw the arm of a bear swing through the air between us and that's what hit him square in the chest and flung him up against the one tree, he didn't miss.

"I didn't need another reason to move. I planned to be at a distance and gun raised before it got a chance to take a swipe at me. It picked up a section of a fallen tree and threw it at me, but it hit a couple other trees instead.

"I tripped over a log, or what I think is a log, until I see it's the poacher's body. His head is flattened across his shoulders. I remember seeing the neck bone sticking out somewhere…it looked so white."

The man pauses, his eyes are distant, the memory does not feel so.

"I drew my sidearm and laid out that beast with all the shots I could put in between its eyes. I picked myself up off the poacher and ran to check on the other warden. He was unconscious and slept until the day they pulled the plug."

Tears rim the man's eyes. He wipes them quickly and took a moment to compose himself.

"As I was standing there, getting my bearings, I happened to see something like a den peeking at me through the grounded foliage. I saw a little face looking out at me."

When the man teared up this time, he ignored them. He looked straight across the table at me, not smiling at me, but smiling at the memory.

"I couldn't make sense of what I was seeing. I thought maybe I'd died or was dying. You were the cutest little thing... all that rusty-brown hair and that sweet little nose. You bleated and put your fingers in your mouth while you waited...you were never good at waiting," he added, with one breath of a laugh, which almost sounded like a cough. "I looked around for more tracks. I needed to know if I could figure out where both your parents were. When I realized you were alone, I couldn't leave you."

"And bear?" I press. "More bear?"

"No...I don't know," he looks off thoughtfully. "Maybe there are other... bear like that, way, way out there. I tell myself there has to be, but it might have been one of the last."

The man told me before that I was adopted. I had to wonder, since he seemed to have reason for looking, "Where mom? Where dad?"

"I had to get the other warden to a hospital. I looked for them as long as I dare. Then I blocked up the den, so you wouldn't wander off, got him help and—as much as I didn't like to—came back as soon as I could. Which meant it was dark…*really* dark by the time I opened up that den. You were curled up, right at the mouth of it. I guessed you'd worn yourself out crying and trying to get out. When I picked you up in my arms, you unfolded and clung to me. I don't think you even woke up…"

"Sick bear?"

The man leans back in his chair, folding and unfolding his napkin.

"I got rid of the body," he said quietly.

"Poach?"

"I told folks we never found him."

"Lie bad," I point. There was no measure for the joy I feel in catching *him* being a bad person. Man, with so many rules. Man, with so many judgments. I felt vindicated. I felt justified. For too long I thought him wrong-less, someone I should try to be like and should want to. But the man was sneaky. Deceptive. A liar, unapologetically. He tracked rain water into the house! He is not eating his supper.

"Eat," I push.

"I will," he returns quickly, "But I'm not going to eat while I'm talking."

"*Lying*," I threw back.

The man leans back in his chair and looks across the table at me. His wet eyes are steely when they fix on me. They are cold.

"About what?" he wants to know.

"*Poach.*"

"Oh. I lied about the poacher. Any interaction I have had with anyone since then, that so much as *remotely* includes you, I have had to lie. You know I have to incase the wrong person finds out about you."

"Still lie."

"*Fine.*"

The man stands up from the table and throws both his plate and pizza into the garbage. I jump to my feet and block the kitchen exit.

"Mad?" I ask, though he had no right to be.

"At what?" he says lightly.

"Me."

He looks into my eyes, his are roiling with thoughts and feelings. With one corner of his mouth ever so slightly raised he asks, "What should I be mad at you for? Can you answer without lying?"

I feel like I'd been slapped. Our eyes lock. I am too dumbfounded to answer.

"No? Get out of my way, please."

I don't, but he shoulders past me. I imagine breaking his neck.

He is halfway down the hall when he turns around and comes back. I reel on him and puff up, that maybe he would not talk to me like that again. He is very lucky when he opens his mouth that I like the tone of his voice.

"I don't know what's going on. I know that you've been unhappy. I know you are feeling things that you don't know how to respond to. I know there are a lot of changes going on in your body…and your mind. I've done the best I can and you've been a good girl, but you need to do the best you can now too, because I don't know how to take care of a bad girl an—" he clears his throat and does not meet my eyes when he continues. "—and I don't think I want to know how."

I ask him why he didn't look harder for my parents. I ask him why I was lost in the woods. I am thinking of how bad I felt, of how confused I felt and found myself wondering how different (or better) my life might be if he had tried harder.

"I did the best I could. I do the best I can. There were no guidance books for this kind of parenting. No research to refer to. It's been nine years…instead of getting easier, I feel like I'm taking backward steps. You're not happy. I'm beginni—Maybe you were found by the wrong person."

That night, I lay awake. That final sentence was all I could think about.

8

I awake in the middle of the night. I have come to a conclusion about the man. I suspect he has come to a conclusion about me.

I am restless. Anxious. I get up. I know what is wrong with the man...I realize we have the same problem.

I stand in front of the mirror, making sure that my wig is on right. I smile at my reflection, my large teeth look scary in the modest light from my dresser's lamp. My eyes look especially small and dark, save where the light touches them—there the color blazes like embers against my shadowy features. I itch at a day's worth of growth upon my massive body. I am naked, until I put on the wig. Then, I feel decent.

The man wants me to be happy. I am unhappy because I am lying to myself. I am denying myself what I *need,* not just what I want. That would make anyone tense, restless, depressed, irritable. The man should be smart enough to have realized that. He *is* that smart. He does not say, 'I want you this way.' 'I want things that way'. He says, we do this in case the Wrong People show up. Sometimes he looks at me doubtfully, like all our efforts are starting to amount to less and less. It's obvious why. I am so big, anyone would stare at me. The last thing we need, the man said, is to draw attention to ourselves.

I am almost five-hundred pounds, unless the man lies. The man is six-feet tall. I am about as tall. Maybe taller, if I stand straight. On TV, all I see is how different I am than other girls. Every couple seconds there is an advertisement or situation on TV that tells me how I should want to be... how I am *supposed* to be. When someone tosses their hair and the camera seems to watch it with the same envy I do, I know. I *know*. They are telling me what to want. What to be. It tells males what they should want too. It's impossible not to realize this will never be me. I could lose four hundred pounds and I would still be ugly.

Why are people most cruel about the things which cannot be helped?

I know why.

We are animals.

It's in our emotional best interest to not care about those who might fall behind and be lost. It's in our herd's best interest to drive out the ill and undesirable. Animals prey on the sick, weak—vulnerable. Animals need to constantly prove who's in charge and make sure no one forgets it. Animals desire the toughest or most beautiful, prosperous and skilled among them— the others are unsuitable for lovers or, sometimes, even love.

We marvel at compassion in the animal kingdom... and also of compassion between ourselves.

The man is not weak, ill, unskilled, ugly or poor. I resent that he is so ungrateful. Maybe that is what makes up the Wrong.

That was the first time the man ever suggested he could be one of the Wrong People. Did I misunderstand? Was it a slip of the tongue? If he is Wrong, then who are the Right People? He's given me no chance to know that.

He's kept me all to himself.

Why?

It is hard for me to walk quietly, even though I put on socks to help. The man is a light sleeper, so walking quietly is an almost futile effort. I know he will wake up if I just walk, so my only choice is to try to be silent.

The man's bedroom door is open. I listen and do not hear the sound of sleep breathing. Is he lying there awake? The bathroom door is open. The house is dark.

I listen harder.

I creep inside.

The man has a few runner carpets and two smaller ones on either side of the bed. I take a wide step over the threshold because there is a squeaky board there. The man installed it a long time ago.

I smell him. I step over yesterday's clothes. The side of the bed touches my leg. I stand beside the middle of the bed, imagining him lying there. My night vision is fair, but the room is very dark. Even on the hottest nights, the man does not sleep with the windows open. So there is nothing to help me navigate, but memory and scent. I breathe deeply.

I cannot tell where his body is. I cannot see where his hands are. I consider his weight; my weight. His strength; my strength. I am weaponless. If he cannot reach one, so is he.

I pounce on top of the space where he sleeps, kneel down on either side of what feels like his legs and sit with all my weight, and as much as I can add by force. My hands scour for arms, hands or his chest that I can put my weight on them too, but find nothing but a roll of turned back blankets. I feel the mattress. It is only faintly warm.

Angry, I spring off the bed. Things rattle and fall when I land on the bedroom floor. I cannot help the angry grunts and frustrated whines. Resisting my voice is the hardest thing the man has asked me to do.

Out in the hall, I smell for him. I listen. I was loud. Wherever he was, he knew I was awake. I pat my leg—dog will come if she hears it, unless she is with man. I imagine him holding her collar and ringing it with his fingers, so that she can't get away. I feel like he does the same thing to me. I pat my leg again. Dog is always in the house overnight. So where is the man?

Then I notice a strange thing.

The man's barn boots are missing.

I am about to turn on the hall light, but I am afraid that, like the lightning, some light would leak outside. I don't think it's worth the risk.

I wonder what he's up to. I wonder where he is. None of the cows are due. I would not believe him if he said there was another emergency call. Not another.

I do not put anything else on my feet. I do not take off the socks.

The door is unlocked, from top to bottom.

I peek out the door, then go out. On the west side of the barn I see the man's lantern. I watch for a few moments. I see the man step between me and the light.

Did something upset the animals?

I don't think so. I usually hear that too. How many nights did I run out into the hall, worried about the animals? The man would comfort me, tell me he would be right back and he would be.

Now, I am sorry that I ever worried about them. They have everything a living thing could want. A home, mates, companions, food. All their worries are tended to by the man. All *their* needs—sated.

I am not supposed to go outside when it is dark.

I go.

The smell of rain is gone, now there is only the smell like earthworms, when the rain has been and the earth is drinking.

It is hard to move quietly on soggy ground. I swing wide. I do not want to approach the man directly. I want to see what he is doing.

When I see… I know what conclusion he's come to.

He is digging my grave.

I throw my head back, I feel the openness of my throat and the fullness of my lungs—I *roar*!

The man almost falls into the hole when he jumps in surprise. He took a couple impulsive steps to flee and found the edge of the hole instead. I can hear he is already breathing hard. I can smell his sweat. He has been working hard and fast.

The conclusion I came to? There was no poacher.

He killed my parents and kidnapped me. My parents were probably his neighbors and that is why he doesn't want anyone to see me. He is afraid they will recognize me. The older I get, the bigger I get, I will look more and more like my parents. I must look like them—*that* is why he tries to change so much of how I look. That is why he looks helplessly when he cannot change my appearance enough.

He admitted he was 'struck by how cute I was'.

I know he cannot see me through the darkness. The lantern light does not reach me. He says the name he gave me. I almost never hear it because I so rarely responded to it, even when I understood he meant *me* when he said it. He said the name with surprise as I burst out of the darkness into the lantern light.

How often does he say he loves me? It does not stop him from raising the shovel between us like a staff. He is afraid I am going to charge. I do not stop moving.

I grab the handle of the shovel and yank it. He lets go rather than sail with it into the darkness. I hear the metal "thunk" against a tree. I wonder if the log that the bear threw at the man made a similar sound when it struck the trees that shielded him. Time has turned the situation on its head.

The man carefully steps backward, over the hole. Mind and body are busy trying to think of what to do.

I straighten the wig, which has slipped forward. I smile at him across the five foot space.

"Where are your clothes?" he asks me. His eyes are wide and fearful.

I answer:

"Man."

I see his Adam's apple climb high under his jaw.

"Gun?" I ask.

I expect, if he has one, to automatically look to it. But he only stares at me before replying, "What about a gun?"

A deep, throaty chuckle erupts inside me. It turns into something like a giggle. The closest to giggling as I have ever been. The color leaves his face. He edges away. I cannot stop laughing. Man is unarmed.

"Up early," I say nonchalantly. I edge around the hole and the man moves away. He looks down at the hole and up at me. He doesn't try to explain.

If he wants me for himself, how badly I want babies must be what has driven him to this. The baby would become my focus and he would no longer have me to himself.

Suddenly he does not move away and squares himself up to me. He says, "STOP."

I do.

"What are you doing?" he wonders.

"What *you* doin'?" I gesture to the hole. I only feel half a smile, so that is all I give. I see the man tremble. He leaps to the other side of the hole. I can't let him get too far away; he is faster than me.

"You know what I'm doing," he asserts, jabbing a finger at me. He pulls it back like he touched something hot. He knows I am sensitive to gestures. I don't always respond the way he expects me to.

"Uh-huh," I agree.

He shakes his head and looks between me and the hole. He is confused. Fear is overcoming his self-control—he shows it. His brow is knitted with worry. His eyes, round as saucers. His mouth makes a tight line and his heart pitter-patters like drumming fingers. The smell of his sweat has changed. There are no more illusions.

It is time for our roles to change.

I want to see what is out there. I want to decide what man is allowed to want. And I want to have what I want without asking. Now that I know how he really feels about me, that he wanted to get rid of me, I do not have to consider his feelings. In fact, I already have far longer than he deserves.

He can either submit or die.

I am not dying. I have only just started to live.

"No kill," I grunt.

"Kill who?" the man stammers.

I straighten to my full height. I am not comfortable to do this for long. I glower down at the man and spit at the hole.

"Kill *you*? Because of that? No, sweetheart. No."

"Oh… I *know*," I tell him. I am stepping toward him. The man has somehow circled so he is between the house and me. He means to run, so I run first! He flies across the yard like a deer. I am no longer running, but chasing.

I spill out over a squishy mass. I feel across it. It is wrapped in a blanket and I can tell by the smell what it is. My own heart is pounding, but now slams against my ribs. My ears are ringing. A clay cold sickness weighs on my arms. My fingers get cold.

Dog is dead!

I push off the ground and run after the man.

How could he?

How could he?

HOW COULD HE?!

I scream so hard I cannot run when it bursts out of me. I run better, slightly hunched. Oh, how I run! Growling and barking with rage and pain, I tear across the yard, following the scent of the man's fear. My footsteps, like the pounding of my heart, is loud in my ears. Surely, I think, the gun is off the mantel.

I push the screen door in, snapping it off the frame. Inside the porch, I reach the second screen door and yank it open. It bounces against the wall of the house and then against me as I step between it and the heavy second door. I turn the knob and am not surprised it's unlocked. The man is certainly standing on the other side, gun raised, waiting to lay me out. I push and can't move it. I turn the knob all the way and lean on the door. It's reinforced—the bolts are latched.

"MAAAAAAAAN!" I scream at the barrier. I hear him moving around inside. Does he not know where the bullets are? Is the ammo on the mantel for another gun?

Then I hear the floor creak, on the other side of the barrier. I can hear the man's heavy breathing. He's leaning against the door. I can almost feel where his shoulder, hand and chest touch the wood. His sweaty hair is leaving a wet spot where it touches, like he means to listen through the door, instead of just rest his head against it.

He is thinking of what to say. I can *feel* that too. How can I feel like I know everything about him, when, until now, I had no idea what he was capable of? Probably, I should be running away from him. If I don't defend myself, I most likely will be soon. He is a hunter—a human predator. I suddenly feel helpless and am ready to hear whatever he wants to say.

"What's wrong with you?" he finally asks.

"All," I confess.

"Why did you hurt Shasta?" he probes in a tired voice.

"No mean to," I say.

I hear him nod against the door.

"I'm afraid to let you in," the man confesses. He takes a deep breath and in a small voice says, "I don't know why I thought I could take care of you or raise you right."

I am about to ask him why he kidnapped me. Instead I ask what I think is more likely; I ask him why he killed my parents. The silence after lasted a long time. I heard the man raise his head off the door.

Yes, I think to him, I figured it out.

"Bad man—" I begin.

"No," he protests.

"Bad man, kill dog—"

"What?!"

"Bad man took baby—"

"Not a bad man," he professed.

"The Wrong, the Wrong, the *Wrong*—Where the Right?" I demand to know.

"There are no such people," he tells me. "Not for you, sweetheart… I'm sorry. You don't know what they'd do to you…but I do. I couldn't leave you to die. Maybe I was hasty, because I was so afraid of what would happen to you, I didn't have the foresight to realize what kind of life I could offer. Or what kind of life you could have. I know what you're going through is my fault. I treated you like a person and that was wrong…"

That's wrong???

So what are you going to treat me like now, I worried. Like dog? Man got up in the middle of the night to dig my grave. He was going to shoot me in my sleep. It sounded like he figured he'd be putting me out of my misery. That's the way people, like him, treat animals.

He didn't *have to* make my life as bad as he did.

"Let in," I rattled the knob.

I want babies.

"I don't know if I can trust you…"

Trust me? ME?!

Blood rushes to my head. My ears ring. I hear small popping sounds. I raise my arms above my head like mallets and bring them down on the door.

I wail, "IN!"

Trust. Trust? I am the only one who's had to *trust*!

"*BAAAAAD!*"

I drive my fist into the door as hard as I can. There is a cracking sound. The wood wants to give. I think breaking bones probably make the same sound.

I chuckle. It's only a matter of time.

I am about to pound the door again, but I let my arms fall limply at my side. For a moment, all I can do is stare at the house, drunk on adrenaline and ego—I am strong enough to bring down the door. But—there is a better way.

As quietly as I can, I slip off the deck and race around the side of the house.

I left my bedroom window open.

I can't tell where the man is. If he moves, he no longer moves loud enough to be heard. Man and I now both have secrets. I think mine is much better than anything he's thought of.

The windowsill is at chin level. I carefully remove the screen, grab the sill and pull myself up. I am met with a face bright with murder—madness and rage have wiped the face clear of frowning, of concentration or consideration. There is only resolve and a little delight. I stare at the beady eyes and long ugly face. The hair is off kilter and wild as the lunacy that makes those small eyes sparkle. For a second, I stare at my reflection in disbelief. Then I realize that I see it only because the man has already been and gone and locked the window behind him.

I am about to let myself fall when I hear the driveway alert beeping.

I hear the man move quickly—he was in his bedroom. The sound of his boots thunder down the hall. He says something I don't hear well enough to understand. If I had to guess it would be one word: "No."

I make it to the front of the house just when the coming headlights fully breach the last line of timber. There are red and blue lights flashing. I know what they are. *Cops* is our favorite show.

If anyone is the Right People, it should be the police.

They need to know man planned to kill me.

I expect the man to be out on the porch, talking to them. Dismissing the reason they came. Making them go away just like everyone else who ever came here.

No one knows I am. That needs to change. Once I am known, I am *known.*

When I come around the side of the house, the beams of their flashlights jump onto me. I hear yelling. I hear confusion. I smile at the officers and squeal with delight. The Wrong is inside, I think. He can't do anything to stop me! I will never be hurt again.

I take a couple steps toward them. Against the brilliant lights, blackness encompasses the officers.

Their voices are jumbled. I see the flash of a cellphone camera. There are cameras on their dashboards. I flail my arms excitedly.

The man would not take pictures of me. I like pictures! I straighten my wig. Another flash. My face, once ugly. My short and thick neck. My arms, too long. My feet, too big. My mass, too much. My naked flesh… tickling with the steady growth of hair too bountiful. They would not take pictures of something they find repulsive. I am beautiful!

I hear the sound of a window open. I look up at the attic.

"What *is* it?" someone says.

Someone is screaming, "Oh my God, oh my God, oh my God!"

"What do we do?!"

I faintly smell man. I smell his sweat. His heart is pounding fast or faster than the officers'. I no longer smell fear…not his. I smell the salt of tears.

I look back to the headlights and flashlights—the sporadic flash of a camera. I feel famous. I will be…I *feel* it!

I hear a muffled, "POP".

THE WRONG